FOUR-LEAF CLOVER

PICTURE BOOKS BY *Will and Nicolas*

THE TWO REDS

FINDERS KEEPERS
(Caldecott Award Winner, 1952)

EVEN STEVEN

THE CHRISTMAS BUNNY

CIRCUS RUCKUS

CHAGA

PERRY THE IMP

SLEEPYHEAD

THE MAGIC FEATHER DUSTER

FOUR-LEAF CLOVER

by

Will and Nicolas

HARCOURT, BRACE and COMPANY . NEW YORK

This is to welcome you
In four-leaf-clover land
Now that the sky is blue
And friends go hand in hand.

"The summer just starting," said Mark, "and nothing to do but sit on this fence like sparrows on a wire. We could use a little luck." He stood on one foot on the top rail of the fence.
Peter looked up and said, "They say a four-leaf clover is luck."
"Let's go find one," said Mark, and jumped to the ground.

They ran to the nearest meadow.
"Millions and billions of clovers here," said Peter.
"Just one right one is all we need," said Mark.

They went down on all fours. They crept back and forth, hunting.

They were too busy to see the bull grazing at the other end of the field. Closer and closer he came.

Suddenly Mark jumped to his feet with a shout of triumph.
"A four-leaf clover!" And he held it up, high in the air.

Startled, the bull charged. And the boys ran for it.

Peter got to the tree first and scrambled up. Mark dodged behind the tree. The bull stopped and shook his head from side to side as if thinking what to do next.

Peter stretched one hand down.
Mark gave him the four-leaf
clover. Peter stretched the other
hand down. Mark took hold of
it. And up the tree he went.

From the branch the two boys watched the bull. He seemed quiet enough. But something in his eyes said that he couldn't be trusted.

Just then an old horse came near, cropping the grass. Mark tapped Peter on the shoulder, crawled out to the end of the branch, and dropped to the horse's back. Peter followed him.

Mark slapped the horse's side and said, "Giddap." The old horse
trotted off. As they rode, Peter saw a dog coming toward them.
"That dog is up to no good," he said.
"He just wants to join the party," said Mark.

They were both right. The dog did want to join the party. But his way of doing it was to bark and snap at the horse's heels. The horse forgot that he was old and started running.

Mark clung to the horse's mane and Peter hung on to Mark. And the horse galloped down the road faster and faster until...

a truck blocked the way. There was no time to slow down. The horse slid to a dead stop. Mark lost his grip on the mane. He was thrown over the horse's head. And Peter shot right behind him.

Both of them popped spang into the barrels on the truck like frogs
into a puddle.

Peter and Mark twisted and turned. The barrels tilted one way
. . . tipped the other way . . . and over they went . . .

and began rolling down the hill. Beetlebung Road was quiet.

The barrels reached the bottom of the hill.
Beetlebung Road was quiet again.

The barrels hit a tree and went to pieces. Peter and Mark could hardly stand, they were so dizzy.

A goat nearby did not know what to make of it. He looked at Mark and Peter with a glint in his eyes . . .

and went for them with his head down.

The boys ran for all they were worth.

The goat hit Peter first . . . and sent him flying into the air.

A minute later he hit Mark . . . and Mark went flying.

They landed on the fence. "Isn't it a beauty?" said Peter. And he gave the four-leaf clover to Mark.

"Boy! Are we lucky," said Mark. "And the summer just starting!"